I Mention the Garden for Clarity

New Canadian Poets Series

This series of titles from Quarry Press charts new directions being taken in contemporary Canadian poetry by presenting the first book-length work of innovative writers.

Other titles in the series include *Undressing the Dark* by Barbara Carey, *The Big Life Painting* by Ron Charach, *Stalin's Carnival* by Steven Heighton, *The Speed of the Wheel Is Up to the Potter* by Sandy Shreve, *The Untidy Bride* by Sandra Nicholls, *Mating in Captivity* by Genni Gunn, *Why Is Snow So White?* by F.H. Low-Beer, *The River and The Lake* by Joanne Page, and *The Slow Reign of Calamity Jane* by Gillian Robinson.

I Mention the Garden for Clarity

by

Vivian Marple

Quarry Press

Copyright © Vivian Marple, 1995.

All rights reserved.

Versions of some of these poems have appeared in *The Antigonish Review, Arc, blue buffalo, Carousel Magazine, Contemporary Verse 2, Event, The Fiddlehead, Fireweed, Grain, The Malahat Review, NeWest Review, The New Quarterly, Prairie Fire, TickleAce, Whetstone* and *Windhouse Reader.* The original version of this manuscript was prepared as partial fulfillment for the degree of Master of Fine Arts in Creative Writing (special thanks to George McWhirter, my thesis adviser).

The publisher gratefully acknowledges the support of The Canada Council, the Ontario Arts Council, the Department of Canadian Heritage, and the Ontario Publishing Centre.

Canadian Cataloguing in Publication Data

Marple, Vivian
   I mention the garden for clarity

(New Canadian poets series)
Poems.
ISBN 1-55082-142-3

   I. Title.   II. Series.

PS85756.A752212 1995   C811'.54   C95-900158-1
PR9199.3.37412 1995

Cover art entitled "Still Life in Moonlight" by Diana Pura, reproduced by permission of the artist.

Design by Susan Hannah. Typeset by Larry Harris.

Printed and bound in Canada by Best Book Manufacturers.

Published by Quarry Press, P.O. Box 1061, Kingston, Ontario K7L 4Y5.

for Isaac and Dale
for Dorothy and Norah

Contents

11 when I was four

12 family portrait

13 I'm told my mother and father
    didn't invite anyone to their wedding

14 Hockey Night

16 When I was little, I wanted a horse named Flicka

17 picture of you

18 (telling you about the fall)

20 This garden is

21 Potion for the first garden

22 What has not been said about the garden

25 Planting Procedures

26 Second Love Story

27 Thorn Amulet

28 of three polite warnings this is the second:

30 Lullaby

31 Questions and Answers

32 Scarecrow

33 Kasimir and Natalya contemplate the garden

34 Map for the journey that takes 6 days

38 mesquite trees

39 what

40 rows in order of appearance

41 for Rosey, who thinks all poets are twisted

42 What if it was like that time

43 She turns him into the garden

44 True Gardens

45 Two Of Every Poem
56 Canada Day
57 four portraits of my sister (for her birthday)
61 Pictures
62 Susan
64 Spring poem
65 a few short years before that
66 Sitting on the furnace grate
67 One of my first memories
68 snappy, bitter, seemingly unconnected fragments
about the carrot
70 I say the prairie may be flat but it is not boring,
71 statements about Margaretha and the cosmos
72 List of things she brought, or, when
my grandmother arrived in Spirit River she had
food, but was totally unprepared
73 hard beings woman
74 My mother meets her cousin on a Greyhound
75 Found Poem
76 my grandmother my grand mother picking the marigolds
77 She wipes her hands on her apron
78 morning glory
79 clothes line
80 Photos taken only in the growing seasons
81 the dust rising
82 The ink instructs the dry page
83 Fireweed woman

84	Sunflower Woman
85	My brother captured the bees in August
86	her breath the texture of carnation petals
87	Do not tell tales about the mother
88	not able to remember her face
89	the name Amelia is on my tongue
90	This is the night you judge other pain by
91	When the earthquake hit
92	she asks
93	There is a railway track above my head
94	if you should die
95	Four or five going to watch the fireworks
96	she said it was the sunday school van
97	tunnelling down into the vast remembered
98	Character Study
100	My grandmother asks me
101	garden witch
102	Chronicles
103	the young crow in first
104	My grandmother says
105	seeking the lost territory
106	my father and I
107	wheat
108	My mother said, in those last days
109	the text is open and wild
110	Notes

I
Mention
the
Garden
for
Clarity

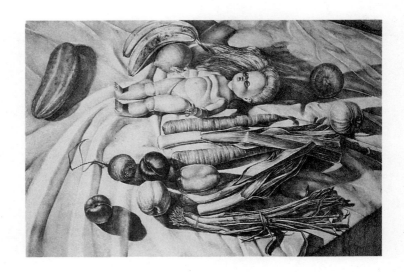

when I was four, when my mother's mother died, my father took us
all for a drive through the valley, past blooming sweet clover and rapeseed
high as the windows of the car, so there was only the straight road ahead,
yellow flowers on one side, pink on the other, the smell of petals
overpowering, my father looking straight ahead, me asking why, my
mother pushing her hand across her wet face *It just happens*, she said,
my father driving deeper into the heart of the valley. It would be a long
time   before I would know   how to get back out from there.

family portrait

How the dead appear unannounced at the portrait sitting, how my brother Bobbie takes up only slightly less space than when alive, making it impossible for my sister and I to stand shoulder to shoulder, how no one wants to stand next to Roy, his body smouldering uncomfortably and his head still on fire, how my mother, smelling of clover, slips in quietly, not wanting to alarm me, not wanting to wake my father from his gaze at the deep oblivious lens, how she carries my oldest brother, still a baby really — see how he waves at the camera with what's left of his arms.

I'm told my mother and father
didn't invite anyone to their wedding
but that my father's friends
put blasting caps
on the railway tracks
all the way to the next town's elevators
and on the first leg of their wedding journey
my parents both got headaches
from the tiny explosions
the smell of sulphur
while my grandmother stood on her back step
where she could see the train go by
dancing and waving her mittens
in time to the shivaree
and the frost was long teeth in the valley
because it was the dead of winter
but my mother wore green.
There were no flowers.

Hockey Night

1

I was born during Hockey Night in Canada.
When the hospital called, my father was cheering and didn't hear.

(This is a lie.)

2

I was born during the laundry.
When the hospital called
he couldn't hear
over the squeak of the wringer.

(This is also a lie
but closer to the truth.)

3

When my mother went into labour
the laundry stopped.
My father took my mother to the hospital,
brought my Grandma home

and the laundry started again.

My father went out to clear the dugout for a rink.

(This is the truth
but my father doesn't remember.)

My Grandma told me.
She said when my mother died,
he didn't know one end of a baby
from the other.

4

My father taught us out on the dugout.
He called the boys 'Rocket' and 'Jet.'
He called me Barbara Ann Scott.

He was doing his best.
He told me how fast
my mother could skate.

5

He aged over night
when he realized Bobby Orr
wasn't forever
but he remained an optimist.
Every Saturday night
he sat in the green chair by the TV.
When someone scored a goal he really liked, he said
"Now that's poetry."

6

He didn't like my English teacher.
When I said Mr Wilkins was the smartest man I knew
my father said "Yeah,
but can he take a pass on his backhand?"

7

He drove my brothers to all their games.
In my memory,
it is all lost sticks and jerseys.

On the way home,
I would look out at the spark of the car lights
in snow on the road shoulders.

My father peered into the darkness,
looking for the goal ahead.

When I was little, I wanted a horse named Flicka and my Dad said *nope, nope we can't afford a horse* but he gave me a runt piglet and I put it in a box behind the oil stove and I named it Flicka and he gave me a kitten he found in a ditch and I named it Flicka and I named a duck and three turkeys Flicka and at Christmas I looked at the bird on the table and said *Oh look, there's Flicka* and my Dad said *Jesus Christ* and chucked his plate in the sink and they say the book My Friend Flicka has been banned in Florida schools. They say this is because it contains the word bitch, but that's not so, my Dad and I know better.

picture of you   in a greenhouse   abundant with cacti,   you
are the young man,   your chin is as smooth as your forehead,   the sh
sh of your smooth consonants   that survive among the succulents,   you
are just a boy,   really,   this is the soft time,   the summer time,
nothing can hurt you,   you think,   now,   ever,   lucky you

We're sitting in the kitchen and I can see the snow covering the ground and
through the snow I can see the leaves I'd been meaning to rake and you think
this is winter but it isn't — not even close.

(telling you about the fall)

1   Autumn has always been the third season: spring tyme,
    somer, faule of the leaf, winter.

2   Autumn: remembering all the places you've lived in and
    the small arrowhead of obsidian.
    (These were the names of the towns: Carrot River, Cut Knife,
    Deschambault, Perdue.)

3   Like spring, autumn is one of the rites of colour.
    Each year I press the yellow leaves between wax paper.

4   All summer, I talked about Zoroastrians, the importance
    of fire and air . . .

5   Quinces among the autumnal fruit are reckoned.
    The autumnal star is Sirrus.
    We stay out late, looking at constellations.

6   I know three women who call autumn their favourite
    season, though I suspect each says this for different
    reasons.

7   Autumn: the grasshoppers and pond beetles caught in
    jars and forgotten on basement shelves, leaves falling on
    the front lawn.
    I buy a rake.

8   When you begin to think of winter, there's Indian summer.
    When you begin to remember summer, it snows.

9   The clothes I bring in from the line smell like the leaves
     burning in the back yard,
     like frost last night,
         a full moon.

10   People never wait for autumn as they do for spring.
     I go outside and the neighbour's son is lying alongside
     the fence. Dry seed pods fall from the vines and leaves form
     a ridge on the left side of his body.
     Slowly he turns.

This garden is
not what you think
it is. It is not
a bean flower
I hand you
but the knowledge
of death, the love
of underground rivers.

This is a secret,

not a corn stalk.

Potion for the first garden

Periwynkle, when it is beate to a poudr with worms of ye
earth wrapped around it and with an herb called houselyke
induces love between a man and his wife if it be used
in their meals.
                    Albertus Magnus, *Book of Secrets*

It's the secrets I want
to share with you
but you draw the line
at eating worms.

You say we will succeed by improving the soil with sand,
by good deeds, acts of charity,
by applications of well-aged manure.
You rehearse the names of garden tools —
shovel, rake, hoe.

I look for advice from the moon, the sun, I sing
to each seed you plant.
The dirt in the line of your left hand is the source,
the alchemy.
The weeds you pull are parables, legends.
Cutworms are potions.

We are both full
of good intentions.

What has not been said about the garden

I

The soil gives way to toad flax
and bitter root.
Even as we eat our salad,
thistles choke the onions.
Pea vines wilt.
Carrots rot.

Nights when you dream
of the copious potato harvest,
sunflowers topple.

Henbane sends runners
deep beneath

our window

overlooks our garden,
the abandoned Christmas tree.
A strand of tinsel
glints for a sparrow to pick it,
glide over black currant branches

and I make a note to remind you
that tinsel can kill,

that you missed that strand
when you took the tree out last winter,

that plants can be used as weapons.
(Henbane, henbone, henbayne . . .
having dull, yellow flowers
streaked with purple, viscid stem and leaves,
unpleasant smell,
narcotic and poisonous properties.)

I wish I was sure
of what we've eaten.

2

In my harvest dream we eat before we leave.
We travel all that day and the next,
stop in the wasteland at the edge of the city,
roll down the windows.
What has not been said is that we love the henbane.

What has not been said
is that finally we are in our garden.
There will be no harvest,
no abundance,
no strawberries this year.

In the morning
there's Florida oranges,
and milk in blue tea cups.
We let the cat out
through the window,
comment on the abundance
of crows.

We tap our eggs
with knives,
talk around the garden,

talk our heads off.

Planting Procedures

1   This is the story: The king's son married the earth's daughter.
She became like all other women and did no more strange things.

2   The women of Sumatra let their hair hang freely.
They are sowing rice.
They beg the stalks to grow.

3   My grandmother rams the cumin seed into the soil,
dares it to grow,
forces her words, fingers
into the angry earth.

4   I plant forget-me-not — "the romance of undying love,"
once, in Siberia,
considered a cure for syphilis.

5   The woman from Sumatra
is like all the others, like a grandmother,
like a new bride. She knows what she is sowing.
She knows what she begs for,
lets her hair hang freely.

Second Love Story

Nettles are the work of the devil. They can also help you to catch
fish bare-handed. Catching fish bare-handed is illegal
in most Canadian provinces. So is snagging fish — impaling hooks
through the body
instead of the mouth. Perhaps you already know this.

Here is the love story. There were lakes and creeks. There were
these fishermen; I don't know what their names were. These were the creek
names: Deerlick, Eunice, Wampus.
These were the lake names: Bigfour, Chip, Crooked, Fickle, Freeman
Isogun, Meekwap, Raspberry,
Tiecamp.
In each creek, each lake that year it was said the fish refused
the bait and lure, refused the rubber, wood and metal; glass.
It is rumoured that many seasoned, once honest fishermen
took to rubbing their hands with nettle.

(The devil wants to know what nettles have to do with him.
He wants to know why this is a love story and not a fish story.
He picks at the scales of the gutted trout,
fights the cat for the entrails, the eyes.)

This is a love story because you love fishing, because you love
rules, because you believe in the devil.
This is a love story because you are so successful with lures.
Do you like these fish?
I caught them just for you. They're yours
if you want them, but they'll cost — paper for love
stories doesn't come cheap.
Neither do those words you are so fond of: hooks, trust, river;
net, tackle, lust; sinker, lake, love; line.

Thorn Amulet

The woman sings "I am the thorn."
The thorn sings "I am the wife."
The wife sings "I am the archetype,
the monster at the end of the ocean.
This is about the devil
all over again."
The devil says
his *Admirable Secrets* —
that man is by nature
warm and dry
that woman is by nature
cold and humid.
The woman breathes icy vapour
against the vase
that holds the rose,
the thorn.
Who drinks from another's glass
will know the other's thoughts.
The woman drinks the rose
water and the circle
is complete.
She sings "I am the rose."
The woman sings "I am the thorn
in your eye."

of three polite warnings this is the second:

The magpie hops from limb to limb
in the crab-apple overhanging the garden.

The magpie hops and
dares the man to end his calculations.

The man talks of shooting the magpie.

The woman tells him eating magpie
would drive him mad.

She says "Leave it alone.
No more subtractions."

The magpie sings
"I am the sum.
I wake you at four a.m.
to remind you that the sun
touches me first,
that the crest of my wing
is algorithm, perfection.

I tell you this for your own good.
It is right that the eye of the woman
should follow me from branch to branch."

The woman rests her hand
on the man's shoulder
but her eye is out the window.

The magpie
bends light rays
to colour
on his tail feathers.

The man squawks
"I have a gun.
I have a gun."

Lullaby

> *The little girl will pick wild roses*
> *That's why she was born*
> *She will gather sap pitch of pine trees in the spring*
> *That's why she was born*
> *She will pick soapberries and elderberries*
>   —Tsimshian Lullaby, Shaking the Pumpkin*

This is the response to words from a song
I never made up.
Why were you born?
I ask this with the best of intentions.
Why were you born and why
did you come to me?
I repeat the first part of the question
so that my intentions
will be clarified.
Why were you born and come to me and
love me and where did this garden
come from?
I mention the garden
for clarity.   I mention it
with the best of intentions.
I mention the song
for the same reasons.
If my mother sang this song to me
it was with the best of
intentions — to tell me why
I had to be born.
What did your mother sing to you?

Questions and Answers

Q   Can garden plants harm us?
A   The tomato can be dangerous indeed.
    Children have been seriously poisoned by making tea from the leaves.

Q   How do I get rid of dandelions?
A   Are you sure you want to?
    Taraxacum officinale is extremely versatile and may be used
    as a salad green, a cooked green, a cooked vegetable, a fritter,
    a coffee substitute or a wine. Take care in making the wine,
    lest you have the unfortunate luck of having the bottles explode in
    your stairwell.

Q   I have a clump of pasture brake overhanging my garden.
    Is there any way to improve my luck in cultivating the fiddleheads?
A   A link between pasture brake (or bracken) and a high incidence of
    stomach cancer leads me to discourage you in your quest.
    However, I want also to warn you against destroying the plant,
    for it is said
    whosoever spoils a fern   will have a confused mind.

Q   I'm confused.
    Why do most gardeners use the common name for plants?
A   The Latin names of a plant are very well and fine but common names
    can be more instructive — widow's wail or love-in-a-tangle,
    for example,   or bella donna   beautiful lady.

Q   Can any garden plants help me with love?
A   The answer to this question is long,
    but briefly stated is something like this: no.

Scarecrow

Write about me,
he said,
standing somewhere between the gladioli
and the onions.
Write about
how much you love me,
how I control the weather for you,
how the possibilities
for happiness
are infinite as rows
in the garden.

Write about me,
he demanded.
Write something   happy.

Kasimir and Natalya contemplate the garden

N

In the market garden, workers trim the swiss chard,
pick the radishes, stuff them into burlap aprons.
The luboks swish their tails and strut
between the rows. The saints emerge from behind the rhubarb.
The hems of their robes are dusted with loam. I kiss their sleeves,
their mouths, pick up the trowel,
ready to begin the thinning.

K

Elemental garden —
baskets of produce
buckets filled with rain water
those children taking in the harvest
Natalya, weeping again,
bending to pick up a shovel

the terrible architecture
of the rows of corn.

Map for the journey that takes 6 days

1   Red amaryllis on the hotel window-sill.

2   A woman, dressed as if it were winter,
resting against one of the combines.
Farmers eating lunch in the fields.

3   Three women on the front porch, shelling peas.

4   Heavy-headed sunflowers. Red soil. My husband,
in the corner of the garden, hugging the birch tree.

5   A map. A road. The man and the woman in the blue
Ford. Lost, just as we are.

6   Lightening that drives the horses out from
under the trees. A girl with a red blouse
running through the pasture. The approaching
storm.

We always take the same journey

a woman queueing socks on the clothesline,
fields of ripe wheat,
clumps of yellow poplars,
Hemaruka,
Scapa, Botha,
Red Deer —
we read the highway markers
until dust is layered on the dashboard,
our arms,
our eyes

There are no maps

I never know where we are going.

He always insists we should be somewhere else.

The instructions
given at the service station
must have been in another language.

We travel past brittle clover,
past a young man building a house.
We travel in straight lines.

My husband points at the distant farmyards.
"The best fields
are on the other side of the river."

Assuming that we will want to go home

We pass through
Madden, Magrath and Maleb.
Theoretically,
we can always find our way back.

Sometimes, as we draw nearer

The sharp suits
of the downtown workers
disturb our memories
of farm women
in grocery stores,
their smooth, bare arms,
their almost empty shopping baskets.

We dream about travelling.

Perhaps we've been here before

I avoid speaking the name of this place.
All the children have red shoes.
It snows on them
when we leave.

What we know for sure

is what we remember.

In this town,
known for its Easter eggs,
all the people walk about
in clean white blouses.

The people who own shops
on main street
turn, as if watching a parade,
to look at strangers.

On those farms,
the houses tall
and the barns with lightening rods,
all the girls
resemble their mothers.

mesquite trees
appear
tap roots
run
through the
garden how
did the first one
get there thorns
the unmistakable
smell of leaves
cooked by August
I say I seek
knowledge I say
mesquite is not
supposed to grow
here the flowers
are pale yellow
and clustered
you suggest
a migratory bird
foreign visitor
ocean voyage
you say broom
came from
Scotland you say
it's how the witches
got to Canada

what
    do you want?

What do you want from me, especially with respect to the garden? What do you want from the garden, in the garden, more specifically, what do you want to grow? Vines or roots, does one fit into the long-range plan better than the other? Do you favour diversification or a concentrated approach — should each row be the same? How do you feel about the placement of seed, what do you consider an accurate measurement of growth? Can you provide me with a breakdown of your preferences, in descending order of priority? In the overall scheme of things, all things being equal, how much real time are you willing to contribute to this project? What other commitments are affecting your time and concentration?   Will you be there   to see   the garden through?

I'm waiting (anxiously with bated breath in great anticipation) to hear what you have to say,   preferably in the next 3 minutes.

rows in order of appearance

rhubarb

peas

spinach

tomatoes and marigolds

(Tomatoes love marigolds. They belong together.)

cucumbers

squash

(Remember to always plant squash in pairs.)

beans

pumpkins

beets

gladioli

(Just for you, though we both know gardens are really for vegetables.)

you, by the garden fence

(You could call this garden an act of love. Hand me the hoe.)

turnips

me, half my face in shade

for Rosey, who thinks all poets are twisted

. . . so I went **right down** into the basement and made myself a picket
and I went right **down** to that garden centre and I told them what I was
going to do. I asked **what** they thought they were doing, selling my kid
passion flower seeds, love-in-a-tangle. I said they **ought to be
ashamed**. I told them they were creating passions that would be the
breakdown of society as we know it. The sign said "**Decent** people, don't
go in here" and on the back it said "This store is corrupting the morals of
our children." I stood outside their bay doors the better part of
the bedding plant season.

What if it was like that time   living in the damp apartment by the bus stop   no possibility of a garden?   Suppose it was like that all the time. Suppose things changed and it was like that again. Suppose things changed and it was like that forever. What if I had no use for any of this garden stuff and I went around all the time saying *Just throw it out. I don't need it now.* Say this was deliberately not about the garden, not about weeds, not about the tendril of your arm. Say it. Say our thoughts were about cities, about the ocean. Suppose it was just like the time we lived above the ice cream parlour, down the street from the Hacienda restaurant and we didn't have a garden   but there was always plenty to eat.

She turns him into the garden. She coaxes the shy boy to Eden. They lie down by the light of the archetypal vegetables. Who knows, who knows what this will become. She composes, recites the elements, fragrances, the smell of tomato leaves, fresh tomatoes, is there anything like that? Years from now they will live in the city, take a trip to the country, a farmers' market. She will pick up a tomato and remember that there is nothing like that smell, nothing like the taste of peas fresh off the vine. She will spend her time in the city, listening to the sirens, wedding cars on Saturdays, trying to remember the taste of fresh peas, the smell of tomato vines, the pressure of her tongue at the hollow of his throat. That was the year she met him, seventeen and seventeen, who knew what would happen, anything, anything possible, the smell of marigolds, nothing like that either, the nod of sunflowers. He crushed the bachelor buttons. *What happened to those flowers,* her grandmother asked the next morning, shaking a piece of raisin toast at her. *Nothing,* she answered, her tongue still unsharpened, her tongue still a soft, buttering knife. The night before, she ran that tongue along his birdbone shoulder. Years later now, she rubs his shoulders, her tongue the knife in his ear, stronger now, her fingers pressed against the knotted muscles, her fingers pressed against the throat of the day. *Thank you,* he says. He is not a birdbone boy. He says more, hears more, listens to her heart beat in the quiet pine bed, knows when it flutters. They are stronger, all in all, but the garden does not compare now, not like the first garden, the garden that made love, the stain of flowers pushing at their backs, her tongue moistening his birdsong collar.

True Gardens

I have to admit that I was trying to come up with a tempting title, something catchy like *I was a hand-me-down horticulturist,* or *He called me a potato martyr.* I eventually hit on *The garden as an instrument of love.* I liked it. Just the right touch. I worked hard to fit the phrase into every day conversation. *Is there anything you'd like to watch on tv,* he'd say. *Something that shows the garden as in instrument of love,* I'd say. *Have a good day,* he said, picking up his briefcase. *You too,* I said. *Just remember the garden is an instrument of love,* I said, handing him his umbrella.

Two of Every Poem

inventions for women: Groundwork

Imagine one woman —

who chooses her landscape carefully:
abbotswood, daydream, moonlight, black ash.
This is, perhaps, the beginning.
She runs her hand across the nursery catalogue

thinking how, when the sun is hottest in the
back yard,

the elder will yellow,

a woman who wonders if there are other options,
on Saturday removes the lilacs with an axe,
digs out every root, stops
only when the spade chips her house foundation,
when knees are covered with the blue clay
rescued from beneath the topsoil.
The neighbours stare between the fence boards,
        eat cheese sandwiches.
She leans her tools against the burning roots,

leans into the warmth of the fire

a woman who does not remember. (Cinderella,
she was once called,
but has forgotten why.)

She tears up the nursery catalogue,
burns the lawn,
puts on the kettle,
waits

a garden unto herself
rock   garden

45

Parenchyma

Equation

Wind twists branches in half-circles.
Choose a landscape
(abbotswood, daydream, moonlight, black ash)
now, while you still have time.

Later you will want to fence the garden.
When the sun is hottest in the back yard
you will want to tell someone
how the elder yellows.

Incantation

Abbotswood, daydream, moonlight, black ash —
remove the lilacs with an axe.
Dig out every root.
Stop only when spade chips house foundation,
when knees are covered with blue clay
rescued from beneath the topsoil.
Neighbours will stare from behind fences.
Lean your tools against the burning roots.

Lean
into the fire.

Inculcation

Put on the kettle. Wait.

(Abbotswood, daydream —
Cinderella, you were once called.)

The lawn is burning.
(wind and smoke in half-circle)
Above the rock garden
magpies split the brown sky.

*inventions of women: R*itual

Imagine the woman,
same woman,
another woman.
You insist again,
again,
what she does is important.
She wants to know why.

She rehearses the right words:
bridal wreath spirea,
honeysuckle,
cottoneaster acutifolia.

She chooses other words:
pygmy caragana
nine bark
mock orange
buckthorn.
She wants the solution.
(she wants)

She imagines you will solve this for her.
She imagines you can.

The Lamb

Imagine a woman in a blue dress
with a scar in the palm of her hand
who sings canticles on Wednesday
mornings as the magpies lift the
brown sky above the careful houses
of the suburb where you live

and she sings your days beginnings
and endings and she imagines
you are wearing a dress of
green and you imagine you're
beginning to like her
just before she sings you away

inventions by women: Journalism

I begin to feel responsible for the women in my stories.
I seek to make them manageable by making them history,
news.

I compose the possible headlines:
"Woman wins award for potentillas.
Woman freezes to death
(digging out of yard)."

"How women are fulfilled
(and lose weight)
through gardening."

I imagine,
but does it help?
Will it comfort me when they insist I join them in the flower bed,
green garden hoses
coiling in their hands?

Quidnunc

The potentillas, the marigolds die —
an early frost.
I remind myself
it is not who she is that matters,
but how I chose her.

The woman, (def: female person,
not a man)
the woman across the alley,
gathering seeds from the rows of withered flowers
into a blue enamel cup,
all morning,
the frost on the trees,
the retaining walls.
I don't care I
don't care,
I say,
but I do.
The geese migrate,
oblivious.

women's invention: Duet

One

    Begin:
    words,
    birth,
    blood,
    burning,
    garden,   teacup, woman, she.
    Insist
    upon the importance of choosing
    a leaf,
    a seed pod.
    Look
    for the right names:
    bluebell, bracken, broom
    while your heroine
    stomps through the flower bed.

Two

    It becomes a question of what should be done.
    She wants you
    to replace the dead child,
    tell about the time she cut her hand,
    blood soaking each revolution of the gauze,
    but you don't.

    She won't tend the garden.
    Neighbours are beginning to complain.
    Dust swirls in the autumn winds.

    Put your hands up.
    Protect your eyes.

Lune

I secure my position by knowing the names of flowers — abbotswood,
hydrangia, polyhymna, terpsichore, by giving you music, lyrics, catvina,
coloratura, knells
by creating, by lying, by irresponsibly inventing women (mothers perhaps)
I want to admire but end up abandoning because I am frightened by the
extravagances they insist upon — blue eyes or political science degrees or
aprons with red borders.
I abandon them on ice floes or on frosty back lawns where I hope that
magpies will come and tear them apart in some fit of unexplained
cruelty. Somehow, miraculously, some of them survive, living in the
underground suburbs, they plot revenge. The wind brings in vague
warnings, portents, slips of paper I refuse to notice. I begin to imagine a
woman, a strong woman who cleans fish, whose favourite colour is yellow,
even though the whole town says anyone can see she looks better in red.
She goes for walks in a yellow anorak, leaves swirl around her feet in half-
circles.

I imagine a candle, the wick still burning, in a house that she passes. I
imagine geese overhead. I imagine a sentence containing the word
sequestered. I don't care, I say, but

invented women: Fragments

Labelling the woman — breast eye ovary cunt — you
would like to be honest for once,
be honest about this, fuck decorum, but can you?
You can imagine her, but not give her a name like Doris,
or Alice, or Marianne. You know you have made her strong.
She will appreciate this,
or so you imagine,
until you dream her angry dreams.
She says This is not enough.
This is not
enough
This
is not
enough

enough

but what can you do?
There isn't room for another stitched hand, a severed nerve,
a ring on a finger,
no room for characterization or grief or a magpie in an alder
or a wheelbarrow.

Look in that mirror.
Watch her breathing.
You may, just before she abandons you,
still find truth in the labels:
vulva, clavicle, tendon, lip,
Venous return

cantle and snick: Riddles and Solutions

1   Begin with something simple —
the half-circle defined,
the magpie unmasked,
the name of the woman,
the wick of the candle.

2   Write two of everything.
Write two of everything.

3   Join, fragment, break down, invent.
Grieve while explaining. Your apologia must
contain bird's wings, bits of string, lunes
(a tune, the moon). Remember Cinderella.
Remember she is a ruse and this has nothing to do
with princes and coaches and everything to do with
pumpkins.

4   Create an ancient folktale. When finished
discard the beautiful woman.
Do not allow her to be brought back by interlopers.

5   Do not always say a garden, a woman. Say
rib rose lilac eye. Learn the truths in magpies, red currants.
Plant them. Let the geese migrate
oblivious.

6   You want just one word
but more is accomplished by listing: abbotswood
moonlight daydream black ash bracken blood
and a blue enamel cup. The woman dancing
with the dead leaves cuts herself,
won't come in for a band-aid, a sweater —
so much is beyond control.

7   Repeat things to tie them together. Imagine
the squawking magpie is a poem. Imagine a woman
woman woman woman. Watch the leaves
swirl in the teapot. Slip
seed pods into the cup. Repeat yourself — again
again.

9   A black-headed corsage pin, flakes of ink from a sandstone
ink well — even the dead child has a name
and autumn is, perhaps, the solution,
even though you've been wishing for spring,

even though you crush each eggshell with a fork,
even if you whisper garlic and rubies,
even when you imagine rosewood, aspen forests to vanish in,

when you start the fire, papers, gardens, crackling,
when it's discovered there are still two shrubs, two flowers,
two candles, two women, two wicks, two riddles
two   rock   gardens —

10   Twist:
My mother makes mincemeat Monday mornings
merrily muttering meaningful madrigals . . .

Repeat:
This is a zither.
This is a zither this is a zither this is a zither this is

Riddle:
The days end and begin and the leaves still falling,
the woman across the alley cleans the inside windows
(around, around
her hand goes)

or is she waving?

Canada Day

I draw the pencil lake and a line running out of it a river running to
Hudson Bay the Old Man River from a cold clear lake at the top of a
mountain ice lake crystal lake trout rainbows I am on the boat down the
river kayak blue canoe fish silent without a paddle I am heading towards
the ocean mouth of harbour I am intent on destinations the lap of water
the cool line of my blue mechanical pencil past the towns of Spirit River
Rycroft Fairview Kinuso on toward the Mackenzie a thicker line the ice
ramming the boat of moose hide grayling ice fins leaping rainbows in the
air I am heading toward the ocean I am in love with the destination I am
in love with the journey the water lap laps against the side of the blue
canoe there is a man on the shore on the shoulder of the highway I am
heading to Ketch Harbour to the ocean I am on my way to the Gulf of
St Lawrence the man waves I dip my hand in the ice water I am without
a paddle I am heading east or west or north if I head south and reach the
border I swear I will turn around ice fish sturgeon I am on the boundary
between provinces I am on the way I am careful not to break the tip of
my blue mechanical pencil water negotiations are difficult I am careful
not to break the line I am on the river the river from the ice cold
mountain lake I am on the crest of a late spring breakup I am in love
with the destinations I am content in the journey the whale in this river
wider than a lake flips a blistered tail frozen water like mercury I am in
love with the destination the boat cut from a single spruce voyageurs pass
me in the right hand lane they are so much faster their songs are sweeter I
do not bother to tell them this is illegal in most Canadian provinces I
listen to the lap lap lap of the water I seem to have missed the rapids and
white water waves as high as houses I am anxious for the destination and
I love and hate the journey I am afraid of the limited lead in my blue
pencil I erase sometimes I see ice even when I am in the Fraser Canyon
the delta when I can see Tsawwassen on the hill the line out to the ferries
when will you be done that pencilwork you ask me want me to take the
dog for a walk go with you put down the blue canoe shake the ice from
my eyelashes never I say.

four portraits of my sister (for her birthday)

Katerina Daydreaming

Sun ripens the flax
in the field beyond fences,

(eyes closed,

your back against a sandstone wall)

I can always find you here,

book an appointment
to view this catalectic watercolour
(Happy Birth
Dear Sis

Intention is every   )
Believe me if I tell you
I miss nothing.
The flax will be dyed,
and woven.
The sand
stone will wear

(away)

The Yellow Woman

The fire is hottest
when you trace the patterns of light
on the blue tiled floor

(resting in the red chair,
almost touching the fireplace)
you brush forehead against your watch,
against sleeve
of the yellow housecoat,

finally understood
colour personified
(Someone has always wanted
this likeness)

The firelight wishes,
burns against you

(to you)   You enchant.

(to you)   You are impermeable.

You don't ask permission.
That is my
yellow housecoat

Ion's Happiness

He puts on his suit
one summer day,
begins to carve yellow wood
in sunlight.

Ion gives you
strong, slender fingers,
smooths your face
with emery.

He hopes, the next fine morning,
to find you picking apples
from the tree beneath his window.

This is a triptych.
By always counting to three
the wind,
his touch
my light words

never reach you.

Still Life

a basket of marigolds,
the woman in the pumpkin
dress
a prairie
in the background
three matrons throw pebbles
into green-bottle water

The wind inspires
their somewhat
strident hair

They are looking past the frame

to remind you
(I am still alive)

(Happy Day)
Are we alike?
You once said we
had the same feet.

This is the final question:
If the pumpkin is
you,
is the basket
(dear sister)
me?

Pictures

of my mother and the runt piglet my mother in her apron beside the
wood stove looking a lot like me my grandmother in her blaring
pineapple tent dress swaying girdleless in a Florida back yard my sister
Charity with a sock wrapped round her neck Murray with the mumps
wearing a beanie my father skating on the dugout a green duffel coat a
fur hat with earflaps silk ties one leg up arms out the pose my mother
calls *the buzzard* Roy rolling on the oil drum like log rolling in water just
before he hits the corner of the shop flies into the garden flattening ten
corn stalks and a green pumpkin Dan in his blue tiger-striped bath robe
spraying a tin can in the lane with a garden hose Rycroft fair Murray first
prize clover Roy third prize cabbage me third prize wild flowers my
father grew the clover my father says *say cheese* Murray smiles Roy is out
of focus my left arm and leg are cut off *never mind* my mother says kissing
the vetch in my bouquet.

Susan

A cup of cinnamon and rose-hip tea,
the ant on the edge
of the window sill.
You see them all.
You are so
perfectly specific.

I mix meat loaf with my hands.
You make scratches in your arm
with the tines of a fork.
The clothesline waves in the wind.
The tea towels are ribbons
in the clouds.
The faded Sunday dress
is a flower garden.
The questions continue;
will the birds keep singing,
will he shoot the kittens?

A song continues
in the simple lines of your body,
the strand of hair
in your mouth.
You stand on the chair
cutting valentines
with kitchen scissors.
You open the red forms
and pierce them with arrows.
You carve your name
on the ragged hearts
in black ink.
It is the wrong time of year
for valentines.

When is she coming back?
Do you like the colour?
Is that a butterfly
in the cabbage?
I begin the apple pie.
You clip a clothes-pin on your tongue.
Will it fall off?

The wind becomes stronger.
The clothes curl around the line.
The ant slips off the sill
to a crack in the frame.
The oven timer rings.
The radio sings.

The questions continue.

Spring poem

the hyacinth too
tulips and daffodils by the flaking porch bright sun bright red blossoms
from ancient branches japonicas quince camellia the dog playing nipping
at the legs of the next-door boy the trunks of trees the fence the bright
light the dog would like to play spring fever I sit on the front porch
remember my grandmother the protective bark splitting away opening
into the spring and sunlight my grandmother opening the box of seeds
and smiling at the geraniums my grandmother bursting into the new
warm air emerging from the house the smell of mothballs camphor
disinfectant sulpha sweeping the paint flakes off the step winter over I am
making a list for the garden centre impatiens pansy oregano chive gladioli
sweet pea seeds I smell alder buds breaking open smell freesias hyacinth too

a few short years before that, living with my grandmother for the summer, sticking out my tongue, because I'm seven, because I want too, because she says, "Don't do that. It's not the sort of thing a little girl does," my grandmother bending down in the sticky afternoon to pull stinkweed from the rows of beets, dimples of fat on her knees, the white borders of what she calls her drawers. "I can see your underwear." "Nice girls wouldn't look." "Why don't you wear overalls?" My mother wears overalls. I miss my mother. "Why don't you get over here and help me?" "Why do you eat lamb's quarter and dandelions but not stinkweed? Why do you wear that hat? When am I going home? When will my mother come to get me? Why won't you tell me?" my grandmother looking south toward the United States, rubbing the limp bangs off her sweaty forehead with the back of her weed-stained hand. "My mother's name was Kathleen O'Connell and she had jet-black hair," she says, as if that explains everything.

Sitting on the furnace grate   comforting metal   colder than
the early august night hot hot too dry this is the dry relentless time this is
the depression over and over again my grandmother hints at dust bowls
and bare closets saved foil and string dry seed hulls of flowers hoarding
everything anything that is useful or precious anything that has the memory
of useful   precious my grandmother the husk of her cough sweet peas
gasping below the porch railing we are saving water we do not water
anything dry land cracks opening in the soil lips around the eyes scanning
the perfect sunset dry bones brittle woman my grandmother panting on
the steps to the basement

One of my first memories of the new house is of standing on a chair and putting my hand in the wringer washer. For some reason, I have no memory of what happened directly after that, what my fingers looked like, if, at first, it hurt. For some reason, I looked out the kitchen window. There were bright pink cosmos blooming in the garden. It must have been August. My mother must have released the spring, loosened the rollers. There were red and yellow gladioli and zinnias and marigolds and the last sweet peas against the fence. My mother loved flowers. She lifted me off the chair and put me on the floor, turned my face toward her. Above me, there was a vase of yellow roses on the table. I think I was screaming.

snappy, bitter, seemingly unconnected fragments
about the carrot

I had auburn hair then.   They said I took after my father,   not her.
There was gust of wind,   whirlwind.   Carrot seeds,   filaments,
brown slivers spiralled high above us.   We were seeding the garden.
My mother was anxious to be done.

(What makes me remember?)

————

I couldn't have been more than four   We weren't even in the new house
yet, but we'd planted a garden.   My mother picked a carrot,   washed
it in the dug-out.   The carrot was sweet and unscathed.   I was artless,
unsuspecting.   This is what I would say now

if someone asked me.

————

When I was older my father would take me to the garden. My hand in his
hand, he tried to teach me to recognize the sprouting vegetables, pointed
out the rows of peas, the spinach.   (I could never tell the carrots   from
chamomile   or grass.

It was one of the things I never got right.)

————

Is a definition in order?

carrot: *an umbelliferous plant having a large, tapering root, which in*
cultivation is bright red, fleshy, sweet and edible.

I don't grow carrots now that I am old enough to choose.
I say   *they are so cheap   to buy.*

carroty: *like a carrot in colour, red; said of the hair. Also, of persons: red-haired.*

They say they are good for your eyes — carrots, that is, and that carroty people have extra bad tempers, especially the women. Everywhere they're talking about carrots, dangling them in front of my nose. They say that they prevent cancer — carrots, that is, not red-haired women. I have a friend who just died of cancer. She had hair that was red in colour. She even ate carrots. I think you could say she was pretty carroty. I guess they can't be right all the time. I always think of carrots as orange, not red. My friend had a temper. It was one of the reasons I loved her.

They say that you can't have everything.

They want to know what this poem is about.
(They want to know if the carrots are phallic.)

————

Ask me. Ask me about carrots. Ask me why.

(What kind of answer were you hoping for?)

————

I meet my mother, my father and my dead friend in the garden. This is a self-indulgent dream or a desperate attempt at finishing the poem. My mother is wearing a kerchief. *It's ugly,* I say. *You always used to be so stylish.* She says *I know, but it hides the scar,* and she lifts the cloth to show me the leafy line. My father is still wearing the electrodes from the shock treatments in the sixties. I hate it when he does this, shows up my nice horticultural poems this way. He's annoyed at my embarrassment. *At least I know the difference between carrots and pig weed,* is what he says. My red-haired friend doesn't know me. She thinks I'm a grocer, tells me she needs a loaf of unsliced hovis bread, some celery hearts. *How about carrots?* I ask.

69

I say the prairie may be flat but it is not boring,

that the woman hanging laundry on the line
symbolizes leashed anger,
that she is the archetype,
evil Eve in the garden,
the goodwife peeling potatoes,
that she reminds me of my childhood,
that she might be the woman
who makes it all good and bad,
the one I have wanted to find
to give me clean clothes,
juice made from highbush cranberries,
explanations for her absence.
I say the towels are a gift to the wind
that sweeps across the prairie,
turns the pages of the guide book.

Stop counting the socks, I say.

statements about Margaretha and the cosmos

She is Margaretha, marigold, marry gold woman on the front porch. On the step is the mustard seed and the cook book. It is 1966. If she leaves now, he will keep everything and the mustard will never get prepared. *I hope I won't have to do that again,* he says after hitting her, holding his striking hand with his other hand, as if it were a chalice. *I only want what is best,* she tells him, never saying that what is best will never be best for both of them.

(In flower boxes, cosmos push their blossoms into autumn.)

List of things she brought, or, when my grandmother arrived in Spirit River she had food, but was totally unprepared.

sacks of flour sugar coffee not enough tea to last
lard candles 16 sticks of cinnamon more salt than
sugar some cotton diapers for the baby   the baby
the baby's needs the baby's illness a fur cape used
to wrap the baby in winter opera gloves worn
under her mitts her husband a hard worker her
husband's desires a picture of her husband before
they left New York looking painfully optimistic
seeds for spring if it ever came the memory of her
mother Kathleen telling her she would be back
before the spring the memory of her mother in blue
taffeta a hat several hats impractical and fabulous
her promising career milliner feathers and hand-
made velvet flowers pink roses and silk tulips
memories of spring netting nests of gauze for
singing larks felt hats straw hats spring hats pins
of lilac and pearl pins for pin curls hats in hat
boxes wild hats with desperate flowers their
elegance blistering the room

hard beings woman —
earth on her hands,
topsoil, garden soil,
returning continually
to the garden, the heart
land, bits of enlightenment
under her nails

My mother meets her cousin on a Greyhound. Irene's a teacher. *Just like her mother, your Great-Aunt Mary,* my mother says. I say I want to be a teacher. *Good,* says my father. *Your mother was a teacher too.* My mother says there are lots of teachers in the family. My father says, *a chip off the old block, like mother, like daughter, the apple doesn't fall far from the tree.* My mother is trying to remember all the names of teachers in her family. *Let's see, there was Gail, Mary, Ivy, Rose,* she says. *Don't forget Aster,* my father says. *Afton,* my mother corrects him. *Well then, don't forget Irene,* my father says. *Goodnight, Irene, my dear,* he sings. *For heaven's sake,* my mother says. *Let's see, there was Linda and Rose and Mary and me, Dorothy, that makes four, Good night Irene, Good night Irene, I'll see you in my dreams.* I tell them I want to teach music. *Good,* my father says, *your mother taught music.* My mother says *English,* but my father isn't listening. He swings my braids. *Yes, the apple never falls far, don't forget Mary Mulberry, here we go round the bush, around and round and round the garden we go . . .*

Found Poem

this   is the way   I first began to think   these
        are the first words   red flower   owl and
sunflower   this   is the dancing woman   these
        are the two robins   this   is the garden seen in my
dreams   these   are the things I begin with
        beans   blonde child   the sun   my mother
        finds me at the garden's edge   after walking in my sleep
        my   joyous childhood   a dream   my
father told me   these   are the first words
        bending to the garden   red stalk   long-nailed
woman   emerging

my grandmother my grand mother   picking the marigolds
mary   gold   golden   marry   autumn   my grandmother my mother   me
marigolds   are what's left   can stand the touch of frost   they are hardy
women living on the farm   pioneer women   women immortalized in
western movies   women who work hard   say little   women who only
scream when carried off by bad guys   when husbands and sons are shot by
desperate men   lacking in morality   and being just   plain   mean   women
who wouldn't have it any other way even when the frost comes early   those
hardy western women planting hardy vegetables peas beans   hardy flowers
scotch marigolds   wearing only simple wedding rings — family comes first
picking the flowers   picking up the pieces   western women   never present
when he says   hangin's too good or   this town ain't big enough   but picking
up the pieces   twisting their rings   gold bands married — that means
something   gold circles   centre of the marigold   if you don't have a gold
band you'll never be an angel   never get to say I'm so happy darling   you'll
wear feathers in your hair   dress in red   work in bars called Dusty Rose
instead of picking golden flowers   marigolds   petals   the smell of frost
on your fingers

She wipes her hands on her apron, cotton rose garden. She hangs the laundry, red blanket on the line, a sign to him, almost off the horizon, the tractor shaking him down. This afternoon, she will freeze the vegetables by boiling them, the green heat running in tracks to her waist. Before supper, before she even sees him, he'll clean up at the tap on the back of the house. House, field, dirt, chores, the shape of their smiles — they have always been divided. If one of them leaves, if one of them dies, half this farm is gone for good. They base their faith on the existence of the dichotomy. They say they are rooted, have the knowledge of good and evil. *(God made the cabbages, carrots, oats, clover, rose bush. The devil made thistle, sedge, bramble.)* She teaches separateness in the flower songs she sings to her children, shows them how their lives will be while she asks the daisy for answers. *(He loves me/a little/a lot/to distraction/not at all.)* If he should leave, if he should die, there must be another he, another one to love her to division. She loves the knowledge of the secret power of plants, whispered by her mother, her grandmother before. *(Garlic wards off unexpected plagues, attacks of insanity. St. John's Wort calms the disappointed heart.)* Always she is teaching her daughter to return to the garden, the heart. Always she is mindful of the willows *(affliction, unfaithful love, betrayed trust, gossiping)*. Every summer she is at the line, the line that cuts directly above the rows of onions, releasing her separate knowledge into the drying air.

*morning glory — a vine having heart shaped leaves and funnel-shaped blue
lavender pink or white flowers*

the power again of the heart, the vine, the hardiness of such a wonder in
this unfriendly climate, the shape of love, we drew hearts on cards and
gave them to our mother, red lavender pink white blue, the funnel at my
ear, all the easier to hear you with, my dear, hear hear heart heat, the
morning glory prefers the shade, if the plant withers, the vine remains
like bailer twine, it is the thing that my brothers will use to hang the cat,
this is the gory part, listen closely to the fading heart beat, the endings of
life, my mother telling me they wanted to leash the cat, lead it like a dog
around the hilled potatoes, all they wanted to do was to leash it, but you
don't do that to a wild cat, a barn cat, a cat unaccustomed to the light,
you don't do that, the morning glory wilts and the vine remains, the heart
shrivels, the funnels and trumpets grow deaf but the memory remains, my
weak mother's song in the sun of the garden, the light breaking her, the
vines at her throat, O choking morning glory

c*lothes line* — *a rope or wire to hang clothes on in order to air or dry them*

the line that connects her to the sky, to the earth, she strings her life out
on the line, pants, underpants, bed clothes, flannel — well into the drying
spring, bras, two dresses, this is not the year when good housewives wear
anything but plain house dresses, aprons, one for each day, Sunday is the
Niagara Falls apron *(as close as I'll get to going,* is what she says) her
messages going out on the clothesline, red blanket a signal, a sign across
the fields, the prairie, that something is close to dying or being born, that
something demands the man's immediate attention, other signs too faint
for him, too faint for the dugout and the girl playing with new kittens
beneath the clothesline — the rope or wire that connects the woman to
the world, that telegraphs her messages, *I will live, die* — *a voodoo lily grows
amongst the iris,* later in life, the girl will read a story where a woman at her
clothesline ascends directly to heaven, this rope or wire is, perhaps, the
line to heaven, jeans, shirts, men's and women's, this is the era when
women worry about which side buttons do up on, women's skirts (for
town days) have side zippers, they are difficult to zip, if you are heavy, if
your body is bursting, overripe, the skirts are on the clothesline too, soggy
wool, they are alive on the line that the wind tips and swings, they are the
reminders of the things that are — if the squeak of the clothesline should
end, all things will be destroyed or lost — this is the one certain thing

Photos taken only in the growing seasons,
my mother insisting
vegetables or flowers stand in front,
her hand supporting a pod,
a blossom. We always
said *cheese*. I never
understood that,
the sun hot on our legs
the dog sniffing everything —
toes, gladioli, my mother's
pickled smile.

the dust rising beside my mother tiny clouds cracks in the soil my brother lost a penny there yesterday my father leaning out of the garden eyeing the sinking dug-out the browning barley I am crushing wild chamomile on the big rock too big to carry away I am careful not to crush my finger I am little this is the little time before we left the old house and drove down the correction line to the new house my mother has to stake everything because of the wind my gardening mother makes dust clouds puffs of dirt rising clinging to her bare legs my father looks for dust devils in the fields I am careful not to crush my fingers on the big red rock with the little red rock fingers stained green and yellow I drop crushed herbs down the crack in the earth I am little I do not go where that crack leads I do not know where the penny is I cannot see the end of the split in the earth

The ink instructs the dry page — *live cure temple cold serve garden history repeat wood origin* — each character a dry brush stroke, the inkwell a long-ago gift from a woman who taught me how to hold the brush, who brought me a silk scarf I've never worn, that sits in a bag in the dresser I insist on moving house to house like a sad memory. The ink block flakes now. My strokes are uneven. I have no one to tell me characters I've forgotten. She gave my father the jade ring in August. She almost married him. Her name meant *Like Jade,* but when little, the nuns called her a 'Christian' name — Priscilla. Her calligraphy was like crippled bird wings. I've always wanted to say that. It was my second experience with love gone. You say these things just happen. I say what happened was a cruel thing. I say things have always been cruel in August, ripe gardens bursting open before my eyes.

Fireweed woman

She sings *new moon, new moon first time I've seen thee.* The clover reeks. The thistle and the hawk are charmed with night air. She sings *new moon, new moon.* Old song, her grandmother singing wistful in her inner ear. *I hope before the night is through, I'll have something given me.* Cures for affliction of the heart. Cures for linear love. *New Moon. New Moon.* Cloves, laurel seeds, Italian thistle drunk in pigeon broth. Cures for the losses. Talisman to cheat time. *Will ye no come back again?* Pyrethrum and ginger in lilac ointment. The clover reeks of ripeness. *Better loved ye cannot be.* Balm of Judea. Cures for the years of morning oatmeal, the man seeking regularity, the man refusing the wisdom of her garden. *Bonnie Charlie's gone away.* She is the whetstone, the wistful heart. She is the weed, after the fire.

Sunflower Woman

If the sun shines
there will be breakfast,
smiles over dishes,
clothes on the line

but what if the sky is
not blue? My grandmother

leans to the sky.

My brother captured the bees in August, froze them in the deep-freeze. They came alive after thawing and buzzed at the summer window. *Christ,* she said, *this is all I need.* It was harvest. We were harvesting just about everything. It was somebody's birthday. There was a cake. There was a knife on the table. *Don't touch it,* my grandmother said, swatting at the bees. *Don't stand on the chair don't shake that present wait till your father comes in wait till he finishes the field wait so he can enjoy this with you wait wait or you'llbesorry.*

her breath the texture of carnation petals, soft, but with a fringe at the throat, her eyes the same, only more so   she says to the girl that she will take her to Grandma's   *to Grandmother's house we'll go,* she says, as if rehearsing   he paces from one corner of the living room to the other   outside the window is the garden   outside the window is the truth somewhere because he looks out the window then   *we're going,* she says, and takes the girl's hand   *over the hill and through the wood,* she says   on the back porch are some rotten bulbs, some rotten dahlia tuber, dug out from the peat moss, where he, trying to keep them moist, has killed them   he is looking out the window, watching them going *over the hill and through the wood to grandmother's house we go the horse knows the way, What horse?* the girl asks   *Is he coming with us?   What horse?   What hill?*

Do not tell tales about the mother do not make her mythical do not try to bring her back do not be needy do not tell us your mother dreams in particular do not repeat this dream: *She is looking for her scissors. She thinks she might have left them beneath the rose bushes. She goes outside without her tweed coat to dig in the snow. "Mother," you say, just as she finds the blade and cuts her fingers.* Do not make the sign of the cross over the vegetables do not resort to incantations above all else do not say *She sows the seeds, one for the rook, one for the crow, one to die, one to grow.* Do not think of the moon the pull of the tides in every body of water in your own body do not look for rhythms never say *Four and twenty and four and twenty blackbirds on the road that day, on the gravel road, not yet graded after the rains.* Never say *Four and twenty blackbirds baked into a pie.* Never sing a song of sixpence never sing a song your mother sang you do not try to make her mythical do not be wistful do not tell tales about your mother Never try to bring her back.

not able to remember her face, finding a picture of her in the garden, rose cotton apron, gladioli in both fists, *gladiolus — little sword, a wild iris, the second piece or body of the sternum* that holds the body upright, that keeps the pain held with perfect posture, that keeps her from bending, picture-perfect, the rigid sword enters and remains, the body remains upright but the stem seeps and stains, this is how love bleeds out, this is how the picture yellows and the iris grows wild, this is how the memory goes

the name Amelia is on my tongue she was the blue woman she was my grandmother's best friend she was the blue-tongued woman she taught me to make bows and arrows from the branches of wolf willows she taught me to climb trees she was not afraid of heights she was the blue-lunged woman she breathed sorrow in with the oxygen and strength out with the carbon dioxide I was afraid of her she was blue like the sky I was in love with her she was blue like the sky like rivers like the bolt of blue flannel in the back of my grandmother's closet she was my grandmother's best friend she took my grandmother's blueness and shook it and the pain came out like stars she taught me the blue flax flowers and the blue writing paper she was the blue woman she was hanging in the kitchen she was not afraid of heights my grandmother cut her down   she was the blue-tongued woman and my grandmother's best friend I was afraid of her   this   was   the one time   I heard my grandmother cry

This is the night you judge other pain by. This is the night of the shooting star. This is the summer when you are not the well-loved child, when there is no family, when the woman who has promised to take care of you locks you in the closet to teach you a lesson, teaches you a lesson, takes care of you once and for all. This is the summer of the northern lights. You think you see them from a tiny window in the closet. You think you hear them snap and crackle like cereal, like your limbs. The woman of this house has made it impossible for you to sit, made you sore, made you see the lights, hear them in a way that you will always think of as snap crackle pop. You stand up until morning. It is winter in the closet and all night the northern lights crackle and pop in your head and it is winter and all the germinating seeds have turned in on themselves inside of you and you wonder if she will leave you in here forever. You think of your mother brushing a cobweb from the clothesline, one of your last memories of her, the clothesline, pink dress, white dress, sky blue overalls, the quilt your grandmother made you — where is your grandmother that summer, the smell of your grandmother, her ordinary table, perhaps you will never eat at a table again, maybe in the morning your rice crispies will be pushed in under the door by this woman who has promised to take care of you, who will teach you a lesson for thinking you are still the well-loved girl. You stand until morning. It is winter in the closet, and the frosty pain is stiffening in the soreness of your back. Your jaw is broken, but you don't know that yet. No one does, not the woman who is teaching you what it is to be taken care of. Maybe no one will know. Maybe this is the beginning of the long silence, when the only voice is the shooting star, falling through the northern lights, into your window. *Girl in the closet*, it snaps, *who loves you now?*

When the earthquake hit, my father, aged 18, serious as hemlock, just happened to be at the coast, grabbed his little brother, five and chubby, ran out into the middle of the orchard to wrap his arms around a substantial cherry tree *as if that were going to make a difference,* he tells me now, says he waited, he couldn't tell how long, watching the power lines, the very earth wave like flax or timothy, while inside the house, my grandmother and Amelia went with the flow, so to speak, watched plates shimmy in the buffet, bibles lemming off the mantle, never completely sure the movement wasn't the rumble of their laughter, never completely sure it wasn't the chokecherry wine.

she asks   she
asks again what was her mother
like   her grandmother bending
to the sweet peas   pinching
the spent blossoms   the goal
is always more flowers   *she*
did some strange things   she
did her wash on sundays   she
gardened at high noon   she
had the kind of skin
that didn't burn   it was her strange sense
of time   that made me think she was perfect
for your father

There is a railway track above my head. The miniature train circles. It is a trendy bar. People say it's such a nice place to go. I think this is the kind of place where you'd grind your beer glass into your napkin, where you'd spend your time looking at the trains and thinking about the crow rate and the CPR, barley and the UGG. My friends would come and shake your farmer hands and you would say *David? Carolyn? How's it going? Oh fine. I'm having a fine visit. My visit is just fine,* wiping your sweaty hands on the thigh of your good jeans. If you weren't dead ten years, you'd have to live through this, would have to listen to the band and meet the guy who plays the acoustic guitar. *Myles? How's it going?* You'd smile, stick your finger under your collar a lot. *Yea, I'm her brother. Yea, I'm a farmer. Yea, Vancouver sure is an exciting place. Yea, my visit is just fine* and afterward, walking down the street, somewhere past the St. Regis, you'd do that thing you always did, after you were confined someplace like church, bored or punished, breaking open like a seed pod, talking fast, talking with your farm man voice, talking about fields or a sunset or the bobcat at the edge of the clearing, that year when you worked repairing the rail lines. You'd talk about trains then. We'd remember our grandfather's signal lantern, how he never went to the war because he was needed by the railway, needed for his codes: *You are entering a station. You are switched to another track. There is a break in the line. There is a dangerous obstruction ahead.* You'd be talking fast, your words running away from the evening, taking me on a long jolty ride into the prairies, where our grandmother would be sitting at the station, wearing the scarf she always wore when she rode the train, waiting with her sunday handbag at the station, just waiting for us to arrive.

if you should die if you should leave me if the garden becomes vicious and the stalks are knives if you should die if the garden should become blood if everywhere against my will blood red flowers should bloom if you should die if the clothesline snaps and all your clothes are carried away by a storm if there is a blight swarms of locusts a plague if the garden is no longer possible if it should happen to you if the garden becomes blood if you should leave me alone with the ugly cycles of the earth like my grandmother one harvest night falling to her knees   blood pouring from the sockets of her eyes

Four   or five   going to watch the fireworks   outside the
fairgrounds because my father does not like the crowds   a string of
farmers parked by the side of the road   mothers and fathers   babies on
the mother's laps   still inside the cars   my parents too   my baby sister
too   my brothers and I sitting on the back   the trunk   I have a new doll
her name is tiger lily   we are waiting for the fireworks   murmur of my
parents arguing in the car   rows of farm cars at edge of the fair ground
murmur   murmur of the parents and the babies cry now   not knowing
why the cars have stopped   children on the backs of cars   the trunks
waiting for the fireworks   one of my brothers says he will throw my doll
in the ditch   one of my brothers says he will throw my other brother in
the ditch   children fighting on the car trunks   some children looking for
flowers in the ditches   way past bedtime   almost midnight   almost dark
farmers by the side of the road they   do not like the crowds   perhaps the
town boys from the beer gardens don't even see the row of cars   the last
car in the row   my father   the farmers   running down the row to the last
car   pinned to the pick-up   the children too   wanting to run to the
screams at the back of the line   the mothers out of the cars now   my
mother running with my sister in one arm   grabbing at me with the other
saying *don'tyoudaredon'tyoudare   go any closer*

she said it was the sunday school van   my mother was
freezing the beans vacation bible school was over   she said it was the
sunday school van   it could have been other children as well as his own
she said it was the sunday school van   I liked the van I liked vacation
bible school the things they showed us in town the swings the soft ice
cream   she said it was the sunday school van   she was someone
visiting   she was a lady visitor picking at the tubs of beans   she said *he*
never knew how to drive anyway   she said we were lucky vacation bible
school was over it was one thing to kill your own children but it could
have been far   far worse   she was a lady visitor   I don't remember her
name   she had a big red ring on her pointing finger   my mother
sighed and shook her head   snapped more beans

tunnelling down into the vast remembered, *on the black sea,*
on a white rock, songs sung by her in the middle, maybe the end of night,
on the black sea, on a white rock sat a hawk, not the beginning of the night,
not between 6:00 p.m. and 12:00, when most attacks, crimes against
women take place, after midnight sometime, when there are snatches of
worry-free time, her child having absorbed the twilight, the night, still
unable to sleep, the mother telling her *on the black sea on a white rock sat a*
hawk and the hawk mewled and cried mournfully, the wind seeping in at the
windows, tunnelling into the both of them, the hawk and owl mewling in
their minds like kittens, like babies, the mother bending over the
threatening night, lost in the story, *because on the black sea something terrible*
was about to happen, lost to the first signs of morning

Character study

In the presence of his mother and Goodie, her sister-in-law, she alternates between making plum jam and looking at the acute angle in the green kitchen walls near the pantry. Half an hour ago, she was asked to go to the store for milk and she refused. His family is getting into the habit of calling her unstable. They ask if she is sterile. She answers by saying she has four types of kalanchole growing on her kitchen table. Constance, the woman with the cigarette, says *call me mom,* asks her if she ever considered being a teacher, says *no one gets paid for dreaming.* She skims the foam from the boiling, remembers her own mother, the green eye and the brown eye, the robin with the broken wing, the mallard that died of fright in the chicken coop, the cat her brother dropped off the hay stack, *to see it land on its feet,* Linda, the girl who baby-sat her, killed on her bike at the cross roads, *it just happens,* her mother said, that night, once upon a time, rubbing her little-girl hair dry with a blue towel, *I don't know why,* her mother pushing her hair off her forehead, her mother dressing her in a yellow dress, weaving her a crown of dandelions, taking her picture with a bouquet of lilacs in the spring, purple and white and purple purple lilac smell, sweet smell, her eyes run, her mother taking her picture with a bouquet of gladioli, yellow and pink, white and red, her hands slightly sticky from the fresh cut stems, it's autumn, soon the yellow dress will be too small for her, the slight squeak of the flower stems as she squeezes them too tight, the sound of the water in the sink, the stain of plum jam on her flowered shirt. *I've never met a woman as messy as you.* Constance talks around the cigarette iced to her lip and Goodie looks down the length of her immaculate in-law hands. She tries to wipe the jam that boils over from the casing of the burner — what are the colours of correctly cooked jam? — crimson, purple, purple, purple, sticky heat, black, *You left it too long,* Constance says, *See what you get for daydreaming.* She sighs, picks up the singed rag from the stove. Later, Constance will tell her why she should have children. Goodie will tell her to run to the store for milk and sugar, sticky sugar heat, purple purple flowers in the lane, drooling vines. She will refuse. *How long has your mother been dead?* Constance will ask and she will refuse to answer. In the presence of his mother and Goodie, her sister-in-law, she will alternate between staring out the window at her underwear on the line and squeezing her eyes into the green inviting angle, the meeting of walls. She'll tell them her mother used to keep the pantry crammed with ribbons and empty seed packets. His family will tell the neighbours they are beginning to notice some disturbing elements in her personality.

My grandmother asks me
if I grew the flowers myself,
the breath of her intentions
watering the air.
The questions underneath are:
Do you have a garden,
as you ought to?
Are you a good woman,
as I grew you
to be?

She will not love the flowers
if I did not grow them.

She will not hold them
until I answer.

garden witch

She carries a hopefulness that no one thinks she is entitled to. She insists her hair is a willow that bends but does not weep. She says that her mother is the moon and she doesn't know her father. She lights the match with the sparks from her words and burns away last year's grass in preparation for the planting. She provides him with fifteen improbable stories about the healing powers of garden vegetables, five of which he has heard before. She puts up a scarecrow, but not for protection. She lights the mosquito coil by rubbing together consonants. She plants rue next to almost everything. She carries a hopefulness that no one else thinks she is entitled to. *What would it take to make you love me?* she asks him, with the delicate knife of her tongue.

Chronicles

She tells the girl   in those days   she pulled her waist-length hair back with
a red-velvet ribbon, brought him water and roast pork in the fields. The
girl presses her back into the white-washed planks, the sunny side of the
house. Her grandmother is planting peas. The seeds have been soaked
overnight in a yellow bowl, the type of bowl they sell at the Co-op, the
bowl they have in the same green kitchen in every farmhouse. Her
grandmother tells her how she used to serve up plenty of fresh vegetables
to hired men, the harvesters, that she always had a garden to be proud of.
She finishes seeding, begins to pick the new, half-ripe rhubarb and the girl
feels the taste of the green stalks, like the taste of copper, at the back of
her mind. The girl wants to forget she comes from farm people, would like
to forget her grandmother, dimples of fat below her dress as she bends to
pull red spines from the earth, cuts the tops with a bone-handled knife.
She tells the girl that the rhubarb just isn't the same — neither are the
springs. The girl doesn't understand that and she doesn't want to. She
closes her eyes and tries to imagine tall, shiny cities, white convertibles,
silk-gowned women. She tries to imagine a man without wind burn kissing
the silky woman on the cheek, but seeds of the ordinary garden persist,
like a dull light rooted in her mind. Beyond her, she hears that same voice
telling her things — soon she'll be too old to work in the garden, he always
liked pork, when she met him, he was a nice-looking boy.

the young crow in first
flight falls into
the cat's mouth the cat plucks
the weak wings the garden

is dry

My *grandmother says*   if my nose is itchy   I'm about to kiss
a fool   if my ears are burning   someone   is talking about
me   seeds must be sown   with the new moon   my uncle   found
me under a cabbage leaf   gave me to my mother   *because*   she
was crying   *My grandmother says*   she has a bad temper
because   she is half Irish   and half French   She is the   heat-
sticky woman   clutches me   against her soft stomach   with
hard arms   *tells me* we're lucky   *because*   our garden used to be
a pig run   *because*   a clowder of magical cats   run   among
the rows of corn   *My grandmother tells me*   we are lucky
I believe her   I   am very young.

seeking the lost territory, the memory, the homestead where he
returns each heart beat, the homestead where he goes with the gun, what is
a gun in the hand worth? He is a school teacher, just like his mother. This
is what I hear everyone say, *just like his mother.* I know her. She is the sky-
tall woman, the rain-maker woman. She visits my mother. I am little. She
and my mother talk late into the night. I hear snatches of her powerful
voice. She says *all the things that we are all the things we leave behind all the
strength all the light.* She is the tallest woman, she bends to get through the
kitchen doorway. She is the school teacher. She is the hard-wood woman.
Her son does the inexplicable, on the homestead, returns to the heart-
broken land, the dark, uncultivated bush. Somewhere in the copse of
willows his father finds his body, face turned to soil. She collapses.
Everyone says this is unexpected. This is the brush fire. This is the synapse
of pain long after the funeral. This is the tallest tree toppling. This is the
beginning of the drought time. I tell my mother how the sky falls.

my father and I
on Sundays, long distance
talk about what is safe
we do not mention the dead
we do not mention the past
the farm dropped below the edge
of our world, the homestead
the heart land, there is no returning
we talk about what is safe
we ask
What is the best garden you ever grew?

wheat

I say he was a good-natured boy and his mother was beautiful. I say he had ripe hair but she was the colour of stagnant water and smelled of rich decay, the perfumes of farm work, her habit of watching the unattainable horizon. The good-natured boy, reaching for the grains of the garden, the mother unmoved, his mother always beyond him, her dank wishes poisoning the boy's blond lungs, the mother to blame, the mother all ways to blame, the father, back bent to a work that is somehow not part of what I say. I say the boy was bright and the mother was painful, like a bullet. There is every reason to blame the mother, but I do not say I blame her. Surely this would not be fair. Look carefully as she bursts open. See how freely she bleeds.

My mother said, in those last days, that he had turned her into a vegetable, never saying what vegetable, never saying *I am a hard green tomato full of bitterness, I've become a cornstalk half eaten by cutworms, you have turned me into a potato with many eyes* I don't know what my father said, if he even listened — vegetables weren't his chore, neither was the milk cow, laundry, children, supper — so many things he couldn't be responsible for. Until the last farm day my mother was vegetables — acorn squash and okra, head lettuce and kale — the garden we fed from. My grandmother never quite got over it — never quite got over how my mother lingered, all those days in hospital, past the time the men called squaw winter, past indian summer, when everything was harvested. She told me years later, out of the blue, *your mother would have been a vegetable, if she had lived. I know,* I said.

(for sc)

the text is open and wild the text is vast the memory uncanny all
the things that we are how we chose how we choose to remember ember
coal the motes and flecks the garden is vast green bursting open the text
goes off into the sunset the word open forming indefinitely what we are
how we came to be these are the first words this is the shooting star this is
night out the window over somewhere this is the garden ripe and uncanny this
is the blush of chlorophyll the stain my mother finds me at the garden's
edge after a dream these are the myths the archtypes these are the garden
cycles my grandmother her daughter her daughter my mother her mother
her mother these are the first words this is the light the O of open the
garden, O garden

Notes

p. 28 The title *of three polite warnings, this is the second* is adapted from the title "Of Three Friendly Warnings This Is the Second," from the Seneca work *Songs & Other Circumstances from the Society of the Mystic Animals,* English version by Jerome Rothenberg & Richard Johnny John, in *Shaking the Pumpkin* (New York: Doubleday and Company, 1972).

p. 30 The quotaton at the beginning of this poem is an abridgement of the Tsimshian *Lullaby,* translated by Carl Cary, in *Shaking the Pumpkin.*

p. 97 Versions of the lines *on the black sea on a white rock sat a hawk and the hawk mewled and cried mournfully because on the black sea something terrible was about to happen* appear in *Ukrainian Dumy, Edito Minor: Original Texts* (Toronto: Canadian Institute for Ukrainian Studies, 1979).

p. 98 Parts of *Character Study* were partly inspired by the following quotation, found in *Anne Sexton, A Self-Portrait in Letters* (Boston: Houghton Mifflin Company, 1977), edited by Linda Gray Sexton and Lois Ames: "Anne's new family now began to notice disturbing elements in her personality. Her moods shifted at lightning speed — alternating between deep depression and extraordinary excitement within a few minutes. Once, when asked to go to the store for milk while her mother-in-law prepared supper, Anne refused to go. She threw herself on the floor, drumming her heels and fists and raising her voice in rage."

Printed in Canada